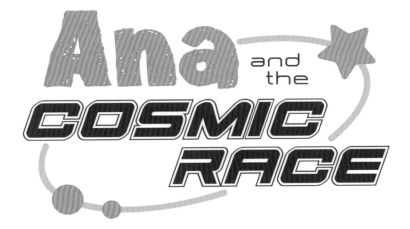

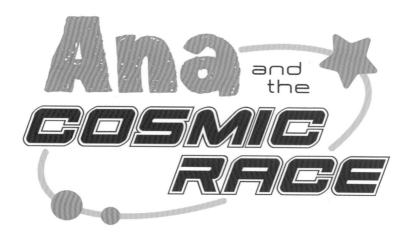

Ana and the COSMIC RACE

VOLUME 1: THE RACE BEGINS

STORY BY AMY CHU
ART BY KATA KANE

NEW YORK

ANA AND THE COSMIC RACE by Amy Chu and Kata Kane
Ana and the Cosmic Race, characters and related indicia are
copyright © 2017 Amy Chu and Kata Kane

All other editorial material © 2017 by Papercutz
All rights reserved.

ANA AND THE COSMIC RACE #1
"The Race Begins"

AMY CHU – Story
KATA KANE – Art & Cover
LAURIE E. SMITH – Color
BRYAN SENKA – Lettering
BIG BIRD ZATRYB – Production
MARIAH McCOURT – Editor
JEFF WHITMAN – Assistant Managing Editor
JIM SALICRUP
Editor-in-Chief

Charmz is an imprint of Papercutz.

PB ISBN: 978-1-62991-765-8
HC ISBN: 978-1-62991-766-5

Printed in China
September 2017

Charmz books may be purchased for business or promotional use. For information on bulk purchases please
contact Macmillan Corporate and Premium Sales Department at (800) 221-7945 x5442

Distributed by Macmillan
First Printing

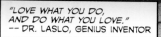

"LOVE WHAT YOU DO,
AND DO WHAT YOU LOVE."
-- DR. LASLO, GENIUS INVENTOR

"DRINK LASLO FIZZY SODAS!"
-- LASLO CORPORATION

WELCOME TO THE PRESTIGIOUS GALACTIC SCHOLASTIC FEDERATION.

ALSO KNOWN AS MY HOME AWAY FROM HOME...

...AND TO 1,247 OF THE SMARTEST KIDS FROM ACROSS THE GALAXY.

WELL, SORT OF SMART.

ZING!

I'M ANA, LET ME SHOW YOU AROUND.

ARE YOU SURE THIS IS HUMAN FOOD?

PLOP

SPLUT

YES. MOVE ALONG, EARTHLING. NEXT!

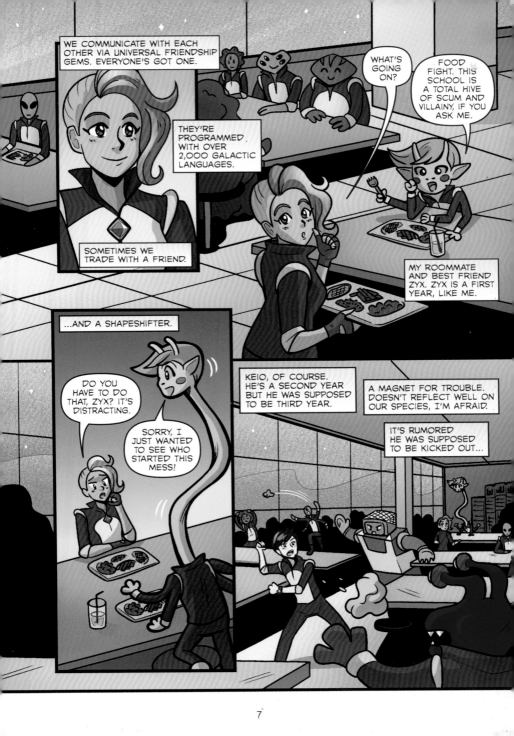

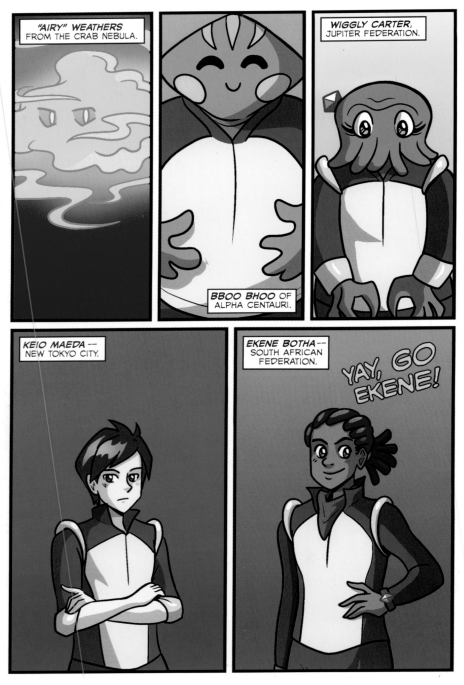

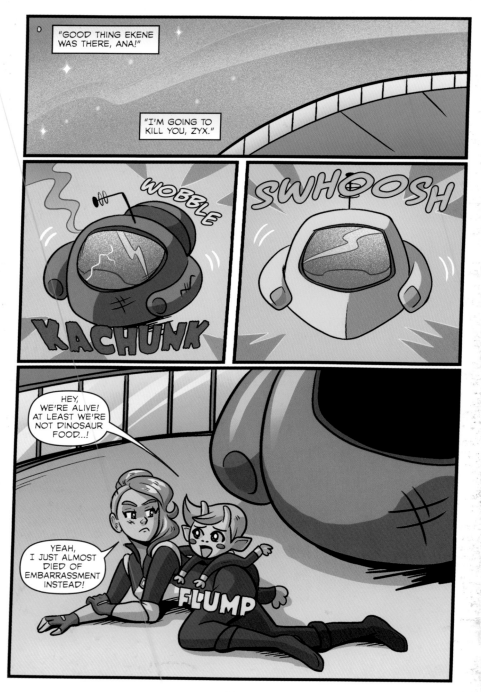

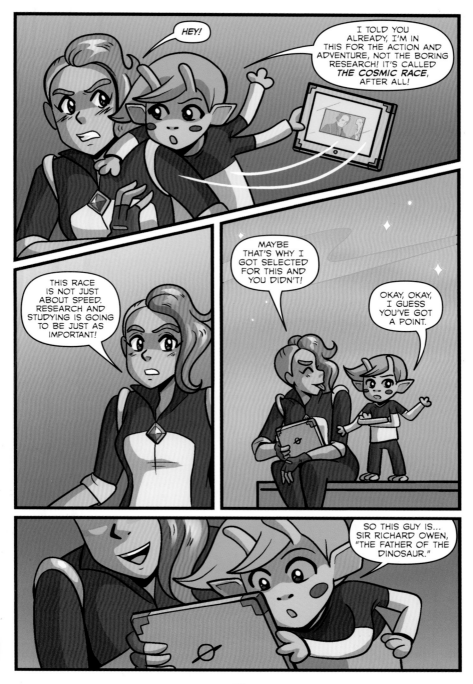

45

48

63

61

74

I THINK I LIKE THIS PLACE. IT FEELS... FAMILIAR.
OKAY, MAYBE I DON'T LIKE ALL OF THIS PLACE.
DO I... KNOW... HER?
UHM...
HI...?
Check out STITCHED #1 "The First Day of the Rest of Her Life," for more spooky fun.

SUMMER CAME INTO THE WORLD FIRST, A WHOLE FOUR MINUTES AHEAD OF ME, DAZZLING, DARING, DETERMINED TO SHINE. I FOLLOWED AFTER, PINK-FACED AND HOWLING.

IF SHE WAS SMILING, I SMILED, TOO. IF SHE WAS CRYING, I'D CRY, TOO.

WE BOTH WENT TO BALLET CLASS BACK THEN. SUMMER LOVED IT, IT WAS HER PASSION. I THOUGHT IT WAS MINE, TOO--

BUT REALLY I WAS JUST A MIRROR GIRL, REFLECTING MY TWIN.

COMING?

GO AHEAD, I'LL BE A MINUTE!

THE YEAR WHEN DAD LEFT MOM. I WAS FED UP WITH PRETENDING. I DIDN'T LOVE BALLET. I STOPPED. SUMMER DIDN'T UNDERSTAND THAT; FROM "US," I'D SHIFTED TO "YOU" AND "ME." IT WAS GOOD FOR ME!

???

THE NEXT MORNING.

WHAT'S ALL THIS?

DAD AND CHARLOTTE HAVE BEGUN TO CLEAR THE ATTIC FOR MY BEDROOM. IT'LL BE COLD IN THE WINTER IN THE CARAVAN!

I DON'T SUPPOSE YOU REMEMBER THAT OLD STORY YOUR GRAN USED TO TELL?

A SAD STORY ABOUT CLARA TRAVERS? I THINK THESE LETTERS BELONGED TO HER!

MOM, CAN I HAVE THAT BIRDCAGE?

AND ME, THE VIOLIN, PLEASE!

OK, THEN! SO LONG AS CHERRY AND SKYE PICK SOMETHING, TOO!

MOM, DO YOU THINK THESE CLOTHES BELONGED TO CLARA TRAVERS?

YES!

SUMMER, WILL YOU HELP ME CARRY CLARA'S TRUNK INTO THE BEDROOM?

THANKS, CHARLOTTE, BUT I DON'T LIKE OLD THINGS!

SKYE, YOU LOVE VINTAGE CLOTHES, DON'T YOU? I THINK CLARA WOULD HAVE WANTED YOU TO HAVE THEM! AND HONEY WON'T WANT THEM, SHE'S STILL POUTING IN HER BEDROOM!

WHO WANTS TO TASTE MY MARSH-MALLOW?

AH! NO-- MARSHMALLOW'S ANYTHING BUT BLAND! IT'S SWEET, LIGHT, LIKE A LITTLE BIT OF PARADISE!

I DON'T LIKE IT! IT'S BLAND!

YES, IF YOU WANT.

91

Don't miss the full story in SWEETIES #1 "Cherry/Skye," available at booksellers everywhere!

Check out more in CHLOE #1 "The New Girl"! Available now!

Welcome to Charmz

I am definitely obsessed with all things romance. It's fun, it's dramatic, and it's all about love. I think love is pretty amazing, don't you? When your heart beats faster at the sound of someone else's voice or the way they smile, you just feel more alive. And terrified! Or how about when just being around that special someone makes you feel like you're flying? Like you could do anything? Falling in love is one of the most incredible feelings, ever.

Of course, love is also complicated and painful sometimes. They don't call them "crushes" for nothing!

Yet, when I'm feeling kind of meh or sad, the first thing I want to do is read a romance. Maybe it's because everyone falls in love, has heartbreak and heartache. Maybe it's because there's really nothing like your first kiss. Whatever the reason, when I want to feel better, I pick up a romance and settle in. Usually with tea and chocolate, if I'm being totally honest.

Which brings us to Charmz, a new line of graphic novels just for you! With stories from all over the world, Charmz wants to celebrate love. Whether we're hanging out in Somerset, UK, the wilds of France, speeding through space, or waking up in a cemetery, love finds our characters and digs right in.

Whether you're in the mood for a (literally!) sweet tale about sisters, chocolate, and forbidden love, or exploring the mysterious darkness of Assumption Cemetery where vampires and swamp boys romance stitched girls, you'll find a lot to relate to.

My favorite kinds of romance are epic, sweeping, and probably just a little bit hilarious. As seriously as I take love, if you don't laugh a little at the things we'll do for it, well, you'll end up actually lovesick. Which is definitely something the girls in our books have to deal with from time to time. Not to mention fashion faux pas, weird chocolate recipes, ghosts, zombie sheep, and puzzles through time and space!

I've read a lot of romances and I definitely have my favorites. I think the one I would take on a desert island would have to be *Pride and Prejudice* by Jane Austen. I know, it's old, but it's so witty, and funny, and real. It's been adapted so many times but it always feels fresh and relevant. Anyone could be those characters. Me. You.

Aside from editing this line of graphic novels, I'm also writing one: STITCHED. This spooky little cemetery book with vampires, werewolves, swamp boys and stitched girls is very dear to me. It's the book I've always wanted to write, with spectacularly weird creatures, spooky adventures, and lots and lots of awkward, splendid, romance. Crimson Volania Mulch is my favorite kind of girl; complicated, smart, curious, kind...but a little bit preoccupied with her own problems. And way too judgmental. No one is perfect! And if I woke up only knowing my name in a strange place, I might be a little self-involved too. I mean, just who is that pretty boy she meets on her first night "alive," and where is her mother? What does a badger/hedgehog actually eat? Do werewolves like cupcakes?

What I want Charmz to be for you is like the book equivalent of a hot chocolate; sweet, maybe a little dark sometimes, comforting, and made just for you. You can curl up with our tales, settle in, and enjoy falling in love with our characters just like they fall in love with each other.

Remember: stories matter, love is powerful, and there's nothing like a love story to make you feel alive.

–Mariah McCourt

Please write to me any time about Charmz! mariah@papercutz.com

I would love hear from you.

STAY IN TOUCH!

EMAIL: mariah@papercutz.com
WEB: www.papercutz.com
TWITTER: @papercutzgn
FACEBOOK: PAPERCUTZGRAPHICNOVELS
REGULAR MAIL: Charmz, 160 Broadway, Suite 700,
                 East Wing, New York, NY 10038